# SCIENCE FILES

earth

# FORESTS

Please visit our web site at: www.garethstevens.com
For a free color catalog describing Gareth Stevens Publishing's
list of high-quality books and multimedia programs,
call 1-800-542-2595 (USA) or 1-800-387-3178 (Canada).
Gareth Stevens Publishing's fax: (414) 332-3567.

Library of Congress Cataloging-in-Publication Data

Ganeri, Anita, 1961-
    Forests / by Anita Ganeri.
        p. cm. — (Science files. Earth)
    Includes bibliographical references and index.
    Contents: Earth's forests — Tropical rain forests — Rain forest plants — Rain forest
matchups — South American jungles — Temperate woodlands — Forests of the
north — Life in the forest — Forest people — Essential forests — Forest resources —
Forests in danger — Amazing facts.
    ISBN 0-8368-3567-0 (lib. bdg.)
    1. Forests and forestry—Juvenile literature.  2. Forest ecology—Juvenile literature.
[1. Forests and forestry.  2. Forest ecology.  3. Ecology.]  I. Title.  II. Series.
SD376.G36   2003
578.73—dc21                                                          2002030536

This North American edition first published in 2003 by
**Gareth Stevens Publishing**
A World Almanac Education Group Company
330 West Olive Street, Suite 100
Milwaukee, WI  53212  USA

Original edition © 2002 by David West Children's Books.  First published in Great Britain
in 2002 by Heinemann Library, Halley Court, Jordan Hill, Oxford OX2 8EJ, a division of Reed
Educational and Professional Publishing Limited.  This U.S. edition © 2003 by Gareth Stevens, Inc.
Additional end matter © 2003 by Gareth Stevens, Inc.

David West Editor: James Pickering
Picture Research: Carrie Haines
Gareth Stevens Editor: Alan Wachtel
Gareth Stevens Designer and Cover Design: Katherine A. Goedheer

Photo Credits:
Abbreviations:  (t) top, (m) middle, (b) bottom, (l) left, (r) right

Ardea London Ltd.: Yack A. Bailey (20tl); Yves Bilat (13tr); Piers Cavendish (24bl); Mary Clay (29bl);
David Dixon (24-25t); Jean-Paul Ferrero (8bl); Kenneth W. Fink (25bl); Bob Gibbons (12bl); Pascal
Goetgheluck (13bl); François Gohier (10br, 29br); Nick Gordon (15br); Masahiro Iijima (18-19b);
Chris Knights (16-17t); Keith & Liz Laidler (14br); D.W. Napier (9br, 12-13); Joanna van Gruisen
(25br); Adrian Warren (8tr); M. Watson (14tr); Jim Zipp (21tr); 9tr, 18tr, 19tr.
Corbis Images: 3, 4t, 5b, 5tr, 6b, 6-7b, 7b, 12tr, 15ml, 15tl, 16bl, 17tl, 20bl, 20br, 20tr, 21bl, 21br,
21tl, 22bl, 27tr, 28tr, 29ml, 29tl.
Ecoscene: E.J. Bent (10tr); Simon Grove (24br); Wayne Lawler (11tr, 27br, 28br); Rob Nichol (28bl);
Dave Wootton (11br).
Robert Harding Picture Library: David Beatty (22tr); R. Hanbury-Tenison (23br); IMS/Roland
Andersson (23tr); 23tl, 26bl, 26-27t.
Roger Vlitos: 4b, 17br, 19bl.

Printed in the United States of America

1 2 3 4 5 6 7 8 9 07 06 05 04 03

# SCIENCE FILES

earth

# FORESTS

# Anita Ganeri

**Gareth Stevens Publishing**
A WORLD ALMANAC EDUCATION GROUP COMPANY

# CONTENTS

*Temperate rain forests grow along the west coast of the United States. They contain giant sequoias and redwoods, some of the tallest trees on Earth.*

# INTRODUCTION

From vast coniferous woodlands in the Far North to hot, steamy jungles near the equator, forests are vitally important. They provide us with resources, such as food, timber, and medicines. Tropical rain forests alone are home to at least half the world's known species of plants and animals, with many more waiting to be discovered. Ten thousand years ago, forests covered half of our Earth. Today, they are disappearing fast. In recent years, deforestation has become one of the most serious problems facing our planet.

*Forests* ▶
*provide a rich food supply for animals such as fruit bats.*

◀ *Great forests of coniferous trees stretch across the far north of North America, Asia, and Europe.*

▲ *Traditionally, rain forest people live in harmony with nature. Today, their lives and cultures are threatened.*

# EARTH'S FORESTS

Forests grow all over the world, covering about one-third of Earth's land surface. They range from the dry, scrubby forests scattered across the African savanna to the tangled swamps of mangroves found along tropical coasts.

## FOREST TREES AND TYPES

There are three main types of forest — tropical, boreal, and temperate. Tropical forests grow along the equator, in South America, Africa, and Asia. Smaller patches of tropical forest are found in Australia and the Caribbean. Boreal forests grow in the cold, dry North where the winters are long and harsh. Temperate forests are found in places that have moderate climates with warm summers and cool winters.

**Temperate woodland**
Temperate woodland grows mainly in the Northern Hemisphere.

**Tropical rain forest**
The world's largest rain forest grows along the banks of the Amazon River.

*Both broad-leaved trees and coniferous trees grow in temperate forests. Many broad-leaved trees are deciduous.*

*Boreal, or northern, forests are dominated by conifers. These trees are adapted to withstand cold, harsh climates.*

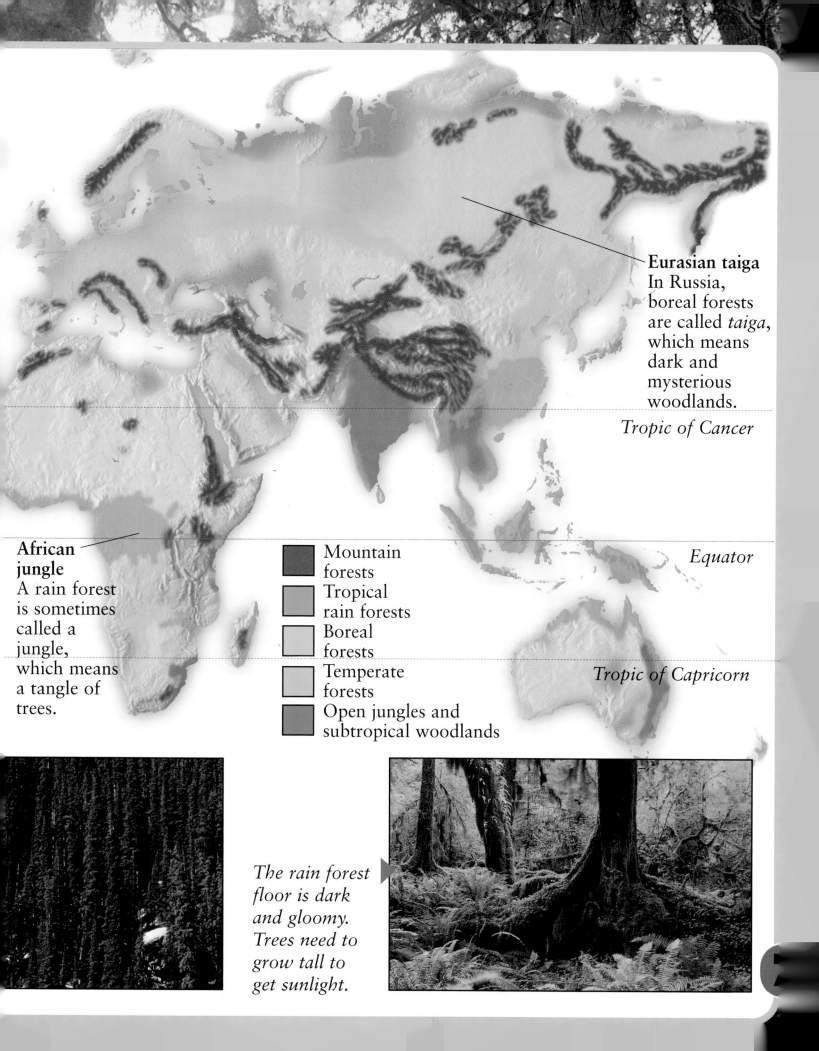

**Eurasian taiga**
In Russia, boreal forests are called *taiga*, which means dark and mysterious woodlands.

*Tropic of Cancer*

**African jungle**
A rain forest is sometimes called a jungle, which means a tangle of trees.

*Equator*

- Mountain forests
- Tropical rain forests
- Boreal forests
- Temperate forests
- Open jungles and subtropical woodlands

*Tropic of Capricorn*

*The rain forest floor is dark and gloomy. Trees need to grow tall to get sunlight.*

# TROPICAL RAIN FORESTS

Tropical rain forests cover about six percent of Earth's land area. There are different types of rain forests, depending on where they grow. All rain forests, however, are wet and humid.

## RAIN FOREST CLIMATE

Rain forests grow along the equator, where the climate is hot and humid all year round, and temperatures average 68–82° Fahrenheit (20–28° Celsius). There is rain almost every day, with frequent thunderstorms in the afternoons. The combination of heat and moisture is ideal for plants.

*A cloud forest in Rwanda*

## TYPES OF RAIN FOREST

**Montane forest**

Montane forests grow high up on the sides of tropical mountains. These forests are also known as "cloud forests" because they are often shrouded in mist.

**Lowland forest**

Most rain forests grow on low-lying land. Their treetops form a thick canopy above the forest floor.

*A lowland tropical rain forest on Borneo*

# RAIN FOREST SOILS

Despite the large number of trees that grow in them, rain forest soils are surprisingly poor. The nutrients in the soil are quickly washed away by the rain. Rain forest plants overcome this problem by growing spreading, shallow roots. These roots suck up nutrients from the upper layers of soil before they are lost.

## MONKEY PUZZLES

The first rain forests grew about 150 million years ago. Ancient rain forest trees included monkey puzzle trees, a type of conifer that still grows today. Small forests of monkey puzzles grow in southeastern Chile.

*A monkey-puzzle forest in Chile*

### Flooded forest

Large parts of lowland forests are flooded when a river bursts its banks. Some shrubs and plants spend most of the year underwater.

River

Flood plain

### Mangrove forests

Huge, muddy swamps form where tropical rivers meet the sea. These swamps support forests of mangrove trees.

*A mangrove swamp*

# RAIN FOREST PLANTS

A huge variety of plants and trees grow in the rain forest. In a patch of forest the size of a soccer field, there may be 200 kinds of trees, compared to the ten kinds of trees in a temperate forest.

## TREE FEATURES

Rain forests grow in layers, with the tallest trees making up the top layer. Competition for light is fierce, so some trees grow very tall. Trees need sunlight for photosynthesis. This is the process by which green plants make food using the energy from sunlight to combine water and carbon dioxide.

*Emergent trees are battered by storms and high winds.*

*Banyan trees have long, spreading roots that hang down from their trunks. Banyans are a type of fig tree.*

*Some rain forest trees have huge buttress roots that support tall trunks. These roots may reach 30 feet (9 meters) up a tree's trunk.*

### Forest floor

The rain forest floor gets little sunlight and is dark and gloomy. It is covered with ferns, moss, fungi, and rotting leaves.

# RAIN FOREST LAYERS

## Emergents

A few very tall trees grow up to 200 feet (60 m) above the ground. Their crowns poke up above the canopy below.

*Orchids and bromeliads grow on tree branches. Their dangling roots suck moisture from the air.*

## Canopy

The canopy is a mass of treetops that form a dense, green roof, several feet thick, above the forest floor. Moisture is trapped in the canopy.

## GIANT FLOWERS

The world's largest flower, the rafflesia, grows in the rain forests of Borneo and Sumatra. It is more than 3 feet (1 m) wide and smells like rotten meat. Its smell attracts insects for pollination.

*Rafflesia flower*

## Understory

The understory is made up of small trees, such as palms and saplings, that sprout in the gaps left by fallen trees.

# RAIN FOREST MATCHUPS

At least half of all the world's species of plants and animals live in the rain forests. The plants and animals of the rain forest community are closely linked, each with their own particular job to do.

## SEED DISPERSAL

Animals play a vital part in spreading plant seeds. Plants need to spread their seeds so that the seeds can find good places to grow. To attract animals, plants grow tasty fruits. After animals eat the fruits, they either spit the seeds out or swallow them and pass them out in their droppings.

*"Ant plants" have large swollen stems containing networks of tunnels in which ants live.*

*Fruit-eating bats help to spread the seeds of many rain forest plants. They like fruits with a musty smell.*

## ANT PLANTS

Some plants have ants living inside their leaves, stems, and thorns. The ants and the plants usually help each other. The plants provide the ants with food and shelter, while the ants attack any animals who try to eat the plants.

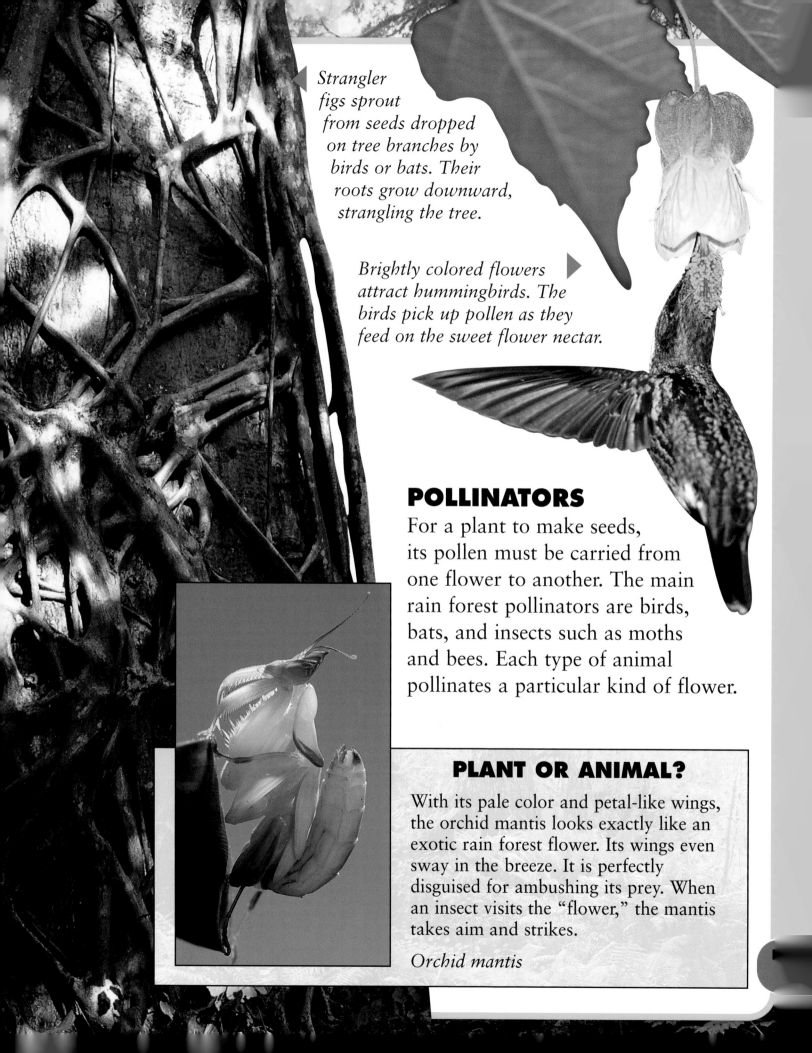

*Strangler figs sprout from seeds dropped on tree branches by birds or bats. Their roots grow downward, strangling the tree.*

*Brightly colored flowers attract hummingbirds. The birds pick up pollen as they feed on the sweet flower nectar.*

## POLLINATORS

For a plant to make seeds, its pollen must be carried from one flower to another. The main rain forest pollinators are birds, bats, and insects such as moths and bees. Each type of animal pollinates a particular kind of flower.

## PLANT OR ANIMAL?

With its pale color and petal-like wings, the orchid mantis looks exactly like an exotic rain forest flower. Its wings even sway in the breeze. It is perfectly disguised for ambushing its prey. When an insect visits the "flower," the mantis takes aim and strikes.

*Orchid mantis*

# SOUTH AMERICAN JUNGLES

The vast rain forests of South America stretch from Venezuela in the north to Argentina in the south. The world's biggest rain forest grows along the Amazon River in Brazil. It covers almost 2 1/3 million square miles (6 million square kilometers).

## CANOPY LIFE

The rain forest canopy receives more light and rain than any other part of the forest. It is home to the majority of rain forest animals, including monkeys, snakes, sloths, and frogs.

## THE AMAZON

The mighty Amazon River flows for about 4,000 miles (6,400 kilometers) through South America. It begins in the Andes Mountains of Peru, flows through Brazil, and empties into the Atlantic Ocean. The Amazon has more than 1,000 known tributaries and contains more water than any other river on Earth.

ATLANTIC OCEAN

Amazon River

Amazon rain forest

Andes

SOUTH AMERICA

*Canopy creatures*
*Sloths are perfectly adapted for life in the canopy. They hang upside down in the trees, gripping the branches with their hooklike claws. Sloths rarely come down to the rain forest floor.*

*River life*
*The giant anaconda is an excellent swimmer, and it preys on animals that come to the river to drink.*

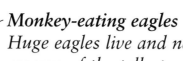

*Monkey-eating eagles*
*Huge eagles live and nest among the*
*crowns of the tallest rain forest trees.*
*They swoop down on monkeys in the*
*canopy beneath.*

## JUNGLE HUNTERS

The jaguar is the most feared jungle
hunter. It patrols the forest floor,
searching for prey, such as deer, wild
pigs, and tapirs. A jaguar sometimes
drops down on its prey from a branch
of a tree. Jaguars are also
good swimmers, chasing
after alligators and fish.

*Deadly frogs*
*Tiny frogs live in the canopy. Their*
*brightly colored skins contain a deadly*
*poison. Some rain forest people use this*
*poison to tip their hunting arrows.*

*Forest floor*
*Shade-loving plants, such as mosses,*
*ferns, and fungi, thrive on forest floors.*
*Hunters, such as jaguars, also lurk there.*

## FLOODED FOREST

After heavy rainfall, the
Amazon River and its
tributaries may burst their
banks and flood the forest.
Low-lying plants may spend
months underwater. When
the water goes down, these
plants quickly grow flowers
and fruits before they are
submerged once again.

*A flooded forest*

# TEMPERATE WOODLANDS

Temperate forests grow in places with cool winters, warm summers, and fairly steady amounts of rainfall throughout the year. They are mostly found in the Northern Hemisphere — in Europe, North America, China, and Japan.

## TEMPERATE TREES

The main types of trees in temperate forests are broad-leaved trees, such as beeches, oaks, elms, maples, and hickories. Some temperate forests, however, contain a mixture of conifers and broad-leaved trees.

*In autumn, the leaves of trees turn from green to brilliant reds and golds, as they stop photosynthesizing for winter.*

## NUTRIENT CYCLES

In a forest, nothing goes to waste. Everything is recycled, or used again and again. When plants and animals die (1 and 2), bacteria, fungi, earthworms, and insects in the soil feed on their bodies and break them down (3). This process transfers the nutrients in the plants and animals into the soil. Forest plants soak these nutrients up through their roots and use them to grow (4). Animals feed on the plants, and the whole cycle begins again.

*The forest floor is covered in dead leaves, which provide a rich food source for earthworms and insects. Plants such as bluebells and ferns thrive in the cool shade.*

## CHANGING SEASONS

In a temperate forest, the changing of the seasons is very clearly marked. Many broad-leaved trees are deciduous, which means they lose their leaves in winter when the ground is frozen and there is too little light for photosynthesis. The main growing seasons are spring and summer, during which trees first bud and then grow flowers and fruit.

1

2

3

4

## GIANT TREES

The biggest living things on Earth are massive giant sequoia trees. They grow in the temperate rain forests along the west coast of North America. Giant sequoias can weigh over 1,100 tons (1,000 tonnes) and stand over 300 feet (90 m) tall. Their bark alone can be almost a yard thick.

*A giant sequoia*

# FORESTS OF THE NORTH

Boreal, or northern, forests stretch in a huge band across the far north of Europe, Asia, and North America. They grow to a point called the tree line, above which it is too cold and windy for trees to grow.

## COLD CLIMATE

Boreal forests are the coldest, driest forests. Winters are long and cold, with temperatures falling as low as −94° F (−70° C). Summers are warm but last just a few months, allowing only a short growing season for plants and trees.

*Coniferous trees' sloping shapes allow heavy snow to slide off their branches without damaging them.*

## TOUGH TREES

Trees have to be tough to cope with life in the cold. Most of the trees in the northern forests are evergreen conifers such as pines, spruces, cedars, and redwoods. Some boreal forests also have a few deciduous trees, such as birches and willows, that are tough enough to survive the cold.

## ADAPTING TO CONDITIONS

Conifers are ideally suited to the cold conditions. Instead of broad leaves, conifers have fine, waxy needles that stop them from losing too much water.

## FOREST FIRES

Forest fires sometimes start naturally, such as when trees are struck by lightning. These fires spread quickly, but are useful for keeping the forest under control and encouraging new growth. Many kinds of conifers burn easily because of the resin in their wood and leaves. Other kinds of trees, however, have developed thick layers of bark that protect them from flames.

*Coniferous trees are grown on plantations for timber and paper pulp. They are planted close together for protection against the wind.*

*Conifers grow cones, instead of flowers or fruit, to protect their seeds. When the weather warms up, the cones open and release their seeds.* ▶

# LIFE IN THE FOREST

Temperate and boreal forests are not as rich in wildlife as rain forests. But the trees provide food and shelter for large numbers of animals, from insects and birds to bats and bears.

*A purple hairstreak butterfly is feeding on an oak leaf.*

## LIFE IN AN OAK TREE

In a temperate woodland, a single oak tree can support a large community of animals. Insects are adapted for living on the tree's leaves, twigs, bark, and roots. Many animals come to feed on the insects.

*The American badger is smaller than its European cousin. It feeds on small mammals, such as squirrels.*

*Packs of wolves roam the northern forests on the lookout for prey such as moose or caribou.*

*Grizzly bears eat roots, berries, and insect grubs. They also fish for salmon in fast-flowing streams.*

## KOALAS

Koalas live in the temperate forests of southeastern Australia. They live among the eucalyptus trees, eating so many of the trees' leaves that their fur smells strongly of eucalyptus.

*Koalas feed only on eucalyptus leaves.*

## SURVIVING THE COLD

Surviving winter in the boreal forest is very hard. The weather is cold and icy, and food is scarce. Some animals, such as squirrels, collect and hide seeds and nuts to live on. Others, such as bears, save energy by hibernating. Their heart and breathing rates slow down and they fall into a deep sleep. They live off stores of body fat built up during autumn, when there was plenty of food around.

*Crossbills have specially adapted crossed beaks that help them pry open pinecones to reach the seeds inside.* ▼

*Red deer graze on lichens and moss that grow on the forest floor.* ▼

*The barn owl is nocturnal. It spends the day roosting in the trees and comes out at night to hunt.* ▶

# FOREST PEOPLE

People have lived in the world's forests for thousands of years. They rely on the forests for materials for homes and clothes, food, fuel, and medicines.

## LIVING WITH NATURE

Forest-dwelling people take what they need from the forest, but they also show the forest great respect. Today, their way of life is threatened as the forests are cleared for land and timber, and settlers from outside bring diseases, such as measles and flu, into the forest.

*The Mbuti people of Zaire are expert hunters, tracking okapi and antelope through the rain forest.*

2. The garden is farmed.

3. The garden still provides food as the forest starts to take over.

4. The forest grows over the abandoned garden.

1. The forest is cleared and burned.

*The traditional way of life of the rain forest people of Papua New Guinea is threatened by the loss of their forest habitat.*

*The open space in the middle of the yano is used for meetings, ceremonial dancing, and feasts.*

# RAIN FOREST PEOPLE

About 1.5 million people live in the tropical rain forests. The Yanomami people live in the Amazon rain forest. They build huge, circular houses, called yanos, in clearings in the forest. A yano is shared by about 20 families, each having its own living space.

## FARMING THE FOREST

The Yanomami hunt game, catch fish, collect wild plants, and grow their own crops. They clear a small patch of forest and plant maize, sweet potatoes, bananas, and manioc. These "gardens" are abandoned after two or three years when the nutrients in the soil are used up. The patches are left so that the rain forest can grow back again. It may take 50 years before a plot can be used again. In this way, the Yanomami use the forest without doing it any lasting harm.

*A Yanomami tending his garden* ▶

## REINDEER HERDERS

The Saami people live in the coniferous forests of northern Norway, Sweden, and Finland. They live by herding forest reindeer, which they use for meat, milk, and skins. They also use the animals to carry heavy loads and pull sleds.

*Saami reindeer herders*

# ESSENTIAL FORESTS

Not only are forests home to millions of plants and animals, they also have a far-reaching effect on Earth's weather and climate.

## FORESTS AND CLIMATE

Huge stores of carbon are locked up in rain forest trees. When forests are cut down, rot, or burn, this carbon is released into the atmosphere as carbon dioxide. Scientists are worried that the release of too much carbon dioxide is adding to the greenhouse effect, which may be making Earth warmer.

## REPLANTING THE FOREST

In some places, clear-cut forests are being replanted. As new trees grow, they take in carbon dioxide from the atmosphere during photosynthesis. Photosynthesis takes back some of the carbon dioxide let out into the atmosphere when the original forest was clear cut.

*Replanting a forest in Thailand*

*Scientists have found as many as 1,500 species of rain forest insects in a single tree. They shake the insects out of the tree to study them.*

*Until recently, exploring the rain forest canopy was very difficult. Today, scientists use light-weight metal walkways, hung many feet above the ground, to walk through the canopy and study the plants and animals in it.*

## WILDLIFE RICHES

For scientists, the rain forests are treasure troves of wildlife. All the time, they are discovering new species that have never been seen before. Finding out more about rain forest wildlife is very important. Research into rain-forest plants, for example, is helping to produce disease-resistant strains of crops that can feed millions of people around the world.

## MEDICINE CHEST

Many forest plants have medicinal qualities. About a quarter of the medicines we use come from rain forest plants. Forest people have been using these plants for years and their knowledge is helping scientists. Doctors are already using one plant, the rosy periwinkle from Madagascar, to treat some types of cancer.

*Rosy periwinkle, Madagascar*

*A chemical in the bark of the Pacific yew tree can also be used to help fight cancer.*

# FOREST RESOURCES

Forests — especially rain forests — are very rich in natural resources. These resources include timber, rubber, food, and valuable metals. We use many forest resources in our daily lives.

## TIMBER

For centuries, forests have been chopped down for their wood. Today, the timber trade is worth millions of dollars a year. The most valuable trees are tropical hardwoods, such as teak and mahogany. Coniferous forests are also felled for making plywood and paper.

## FOOD FROM THE RAIN FORESTS

Many of the foods we buy at the supermarket come from rain forests. Foods grown in rain forests include fruit, such as bananas and pineapples; nuts, such as Brazil nuts; and spices, such as pepper, ginger, and cloves. The beans used to make coffee and chocolate are the seeds of rain forest trees.

*A worker picking coffee beans*
▼

Coffee

Lychees

Bananas

Cashews

Black pepper

Mango

Brazil nuts

Figs

Papaya

*People get rubber from trees like these by making cuts in their bark. The sticky latex oozes out and drips into collecting bowls.*

*Almost all of the coniferous forests of western North America have been felled for timber. These redwood logs are being floated downriver to be cut at a sawmill.*

## RUBBER TAPPING

Rubber is made from the white, sticky sap, called latex, from rain forest rubber trees. Most of the world's rubber comes from huge plantations in Southeast Asia.

Avocado

Kiwano

Passion fruit

## PRECIOUS METALS

Some rain forests are rich in valuable metals such as gold, aluminum, iron, copper, and manganese. But large-scale mining destroys huge areas of rain forest and pollutes the land. Roads built to transport miners and equipment also leave scars on the landscape.

*A mine in Papua New Guinea*

# FORESTS IN DANGER

All over the world, forests are being cut down. It is not only the rain forests that are in danger. The boreal forests and the temperate woodlands are also vanishing.

## FOREST CLEARANCE

Forests are cut down for many reasons, including for their timber and to clear land for farming and cattle ranching. Vast areas of Central American rain forest have been cleared for cattle ranching. Most of the beef produced there is made into burgers in the United States.

*Orangutan*

*Large areas of forest are cut down with the help of machinery.*

*Tiger*

*Gorilla*

# FORESTS IN THE FUTURE

Saving the forests and their precious resources has become one of the most urgent environmental concerns facing us today. All over the world, conservation groups and governments are working to halt the destruction. In some countries, forests have been made into national parks where logging, mining, and hunting are banned. Replanting programs have been started in some poorer countries in which wood from the forests is a vital source of fuel.

*Land cleared for cattle ranching is only productive for a few years. Then the ranch has to be moved and another area of forest has to be cleared.*

*When there are no tree roots to bind the soil together on a hillside, a landslide can occur.*

# AMAZING FACTS

| | |
|---|---|
| LARGEST FOREST | The largest forest in the world is the vast boreal forest that stretches across the far north of North America, Russia, and Europe. In places, it measures over 1,200 miles (2,000 km) wide, and it is over 6,200 miles (10,000 km) from one end to the other. |
| BIGGEST RAINFOREST | The biggest rain forest is the Amazon rain forest in Brazil. It covers almost 2 1/3 million square miles (6 million sq km). This forest is being destroyed at an alarming rate. Experts estimate that a piece of forest the size of Switzerland is being cut down every year. At this rate, in 30–50 years the Amazon rain forest could be gone. |
| WETTEST FORESTS | In most rain forests, rain falls almost every day in heavy afternoon downpours, totaling about 71 inches (1,800 millimeters) of rain a year. The heaviest rainfall on record occurs in the forests of Liberia, in Africa, where rain can fall at 250 miles (400 km) an hour. |
| LARGEST MANGROVE FOREST | The Sundarbans stretch for about 160 miles (260 km) along the coast of the Bay of Bengal in India and Bangladesh. They are the largest mangrove forest in the world. The Sundarbans are one of the last remaining habitats of the rare Bengal tiger. |
| LARGEST TREE | Giant sequoias, which are coniferous trees, are the most massive living things in the world. The largest is a tree called the General Sherman, located in California's Sequoia National Park. It stands over 310 feet (95 m) tall and measures more than 82 feet (25 m) around its trunk. It weighs an enormous 6,600 tons (6,000 tonnes). |
| RAREST FOREST ANIMALS | Among the rarest forest mammals are giant pandas. There may be only about 800 pandas left in the wild. Giant pandas live in patches of mountain forest in China and feed on the bamboo that grows there. |
| WORST FOREST FIRES | In summer 1997, farmers in Indonesia lit fires to clear farmland. But the fires quickly spread out of control, destroying vast areas of rain forest. The fires raged for months, covering the region with a thick cloud of smoke. Thousands of firefighters struggled to put out the flames. |

# GLOSSARY

**boreal:** having to do with northern areas.

**broad-leaved:** having flat, wide leaves that fall off in winter.

**deciduous:** having parts that fall off in a certain season, as some trees lose their leaves in the winter.

**deforestation:** the cutting down of forests.

**evergreens:** trees that keep their leaves all year round.

**greenhouse effect:** the way gases in Earth's atmosphere, such as carbon dioxide, trap the Sun's heat, causing Earth's surface to warm up.

**manioc:** a plant with potato-like tubers used to make flour, bread, and beer.

**photosynthesis:** the process by which plants make their own food using the energy from sunlight to combine carbon dioxide and water.

**plantations:** large forests of trees that have been planted like fields of crops.

**pollination:** the moving of pollen from a male flower or flower part to a female flower or flower part so a seed can grow.

**prey:** animals that are hunted for food.

**savanna:** a grassland with scattered trees.

**taiga:** boreal forest land in northern Russia that contains mostly coniferous trees.

**tributaries:** smaller rivers and streams that flow into a main river.

# MORE BOOKS TO READ

*Forest Scientists. Scientists of the Biomes* series. Chuck Miller (Raintree Steck-Vaughan Publishers)

*Journey into the Rainforest.* Tim Knight (Oxford University Press Childrens Books)

*Smithsonian Handbooks: Trees.* Allen J. Coombes (DK Publishing)

*Take a Tree Walk.* Jane Kirkland (Stillwater Publishing)

# WEB SITES

Deciduous Forest
*http://www. blueplanetbiomes.org/ deciduous_forest.htm*

Forests.org
*http://forest.org/links/Forest_Information/ For_Kids/*

Due to the dynamic nature of the Internet, some web sites stay current longer than others. To find additional web sites, use a reliable search engine with one or more of the following keywords: *Amazon, boreal forests, conifers, deforestation, giant sequoias, rain forests, rubber, taiga, Yanomami.*

# INDEX